HUNDRED WORD HORROR

Compiled & edited by A.R. Ward

Hundred Word Horror: Home

A Ghost Orchid Press Anthology

First published in Great Britain 2021 by Ghost Orchid Press

ISBN (paperback): 978-1-8383915-0-8

ISBN (e-book): 978-1-8383915-1-5

Cover design and book formatting by Claire Saag

Cover image © chainatp via Canva.com

Illustrations from Vintage Illustrations via Canva.com

One need not be a chamber to be haunted,
One need not be a house;
The brain has corridors surpassing
Material place.

Far safer, of a midnight meeting
External ghost,
Than an interior confronting
That whiter host.

Far safer through an Abbey gallop,
The stones achase,
Than, moonless, one's own self encounter
In lonesome place.

Ourself, behind ourself concealed,
Should startle most;
Assassin, hid in our apartment,
Be horror's least.

The prudent carries a revolver,
He bolts the door,
O'erlooking a superior spectre
More near.

Emily Dickinson

CONTENTS

FOREWORD

Home. A place of sanctuary. A place of calm and comfort. And sometimes, a place of hidden darkness. What secrets lie beneath the cosy façade of suburbia? What ghosts lurk in the hallways of an abandoned family home? A house carries memories in its walls: the lives and deaths of its inhabitants are woven into its fabric. If it could speak, what stories might it tell?

And of course, 'Home' doesn't always mean a house. Not if you're a burrowing parasite, or a baby nestled in its mother's womb. Home can be a shifting thing: a feeling, or a person. The stories and poetry in this collection—all expertly crafted in precisely one hundred words—will challenge your expectations, shock, amuse, and terrify you.

So don't be shy. You're most welcome here. Please, step inside, take a look around.

Make yourself at home.

A.R. Ward

WELCOME HOME

1

Priced to Sell
by J.R. Handfield

Don't miss this exciting opportunity! Cosy, historic colonial minutes from the city. Quiet, rustic location with nearby amenities. (DISCLOSURE: Walls bleed.) A modern playground within walking distance for your children. Home is move-in ready, with water, sewer, and natural gas. (DISCLOSURE: Prior owner disembowelled in basement by The Creature.) The spacious eat-in kitchen features an island, stainless steel appliances, and classic oak cabinets. (DISCLOSURE: Oven Demon has taste for toddlers.) A great room for entertaining, five bedrooms, and three bathrooms. (DISCLOSURE: Closet Goblin provides/removes family members as needed.)

Priced to sell - don't miss this once-in-a-lifetime chance for home ownership!

J.R. HANDFIELD (@jrhandfield on Twitter) lives in Central Massachusetts with his wife, his son, and his cat; not necessarily in that order.

2

A Heart to Every Home
by Mary Rajotte

There is a heart to every home, but it can wither without care.

Sometimes it is snuffed out by old hurts. Other times, it lingers bewildered on the wind. Or dims like a fleeting memory.

You can hear its pulse in the dreadful moments of stone-cold silence and in the dead of night when the telltale echo of a life once lived thrums in a low, dull, quick sound.

There is a heart to every home. Mine pulses from beneath the very foundation. Louder, louder, louder. But like a secret yearning to be heard, I moulder and waste away.

Toronto-native MARY RAJOTTE has a penchant for penning nightmarish tales of folk horror and paranormal suspense. Her work has been published in Shroud Magazine, The Library of Horror Press, *the* Great Lakes Horror Company, Magnificent Cowlick Media, Fabled Collective *and* Burial Day Books. *Sometimes camera-elusive but always coffee-fuelled, you can find Mary at her website maryrajotte.com or support her Patreon for exclusive fiction at patreon.com/maryrajotte.*

3

Housewarming
by K.M. Bennett

I shivered on the cold porch, lowering the shiny gold package. Heat, I thought to myself, is what makes a home welcoming. Imagining the nice couple slumbering in their toasty bed made me smile. I met them during an open house for this place. Even though they narrowly outbid me for the 2,000-square-foot ranch, I'll still leave a housewarming gift. Our town has standards to uphold. They will find the gift in the morning and realise this. Driving away, I warm my cold bones with the thought of the explosion that will ignite the house when the bomb is opened.

K.M. BENNETT's work has appeared in several anthologies, including the Daughters of Darkness *all-women horror anthology. Her work has also been produced on multiple podcasts, including the* NoSleep Podcast *and* ManaWaker Flash Fiction *podcast. You can learn more at ThatKatieLady.com or by following @That_Katie_Lady on Twitter.*

4

Le Petit House of Fine Blood and Brain Matter by Michael Anthony Dioguardi

The secret ingredient, my love? That would be your brains, of course. Doused in haemoglobin sauce and sautéed in spinal puree! It's just simply delicious, or as the reanimated French would say, *sang savoureux*! Sit down and let my waiter gnaw at your skull while I uncage my busboys; they've been rotting at the core while waiting. At *Le Petit House of Fine Blood and Brain Matter*, you are always the special of the day! About the payment, how could I forget? We accept temporal lobes and brain stems. And you've brought a guest! How kind of you. *Bon appétit*!

MICHAEL ANTHONY DIOGUARDI teaches and writes in upstate New York. Links to more of his published work can be found here: https://michaeldioguardisciencefiction.tumblr.com/

5

A Place for Everything, and Everything in Its Place by Sarah Jackson

Anita sat alone in her flat for the first time, surrounded by boxes.

She'd unpacked a little before sinking into the sofa, enjoyed the sounds of her belongings settling in: the clink of glasses in the cupboard, the jangle of cutlery in the drawer. Each a tiny fanfare for her freedom. She listened to the beautiful silence. No screaming. No slamming doors. She allowed herself a small triumphant smile.

Heading back to the kitchen, she stopped in the doorway with a gasp. The worktop bristled with her cutlery, jammed an inch deep into the polished granite. It had followed her.

SARAH JACKSON loves ghosts of all kinds: scary, sad, friendly, angry, in a house, on a ship, in your head. All good. She wrote a history book about socialist suffragettes and founded a museum with a friend. In her day job, she helps charities improve their words and websites. You can find her at sarahijackson.com.

6

The Newly-Weds' First Home
by K.J. Watson

Determined to give my new wife a house she'd adore, I decorated the hall with bespoke art.

'Do we want your taxidermic parents glaring at us each time we come home?' my bride asked. 'Couldn't you have had a pair of were-wolves stuffed instead?'

I fared no better with the furnishings for our bedroom.

'We should have memory foam, not coiled springs, in the king-size coffin,' she declared.

In the kitchen, I had greater success.

'Darling,' she crooned. 'That furnace, the two-metre chopping board and the rack of bone saws are perfect. I sense we're going to be happy here.'

K. J. WATSON's fiction has appeared on the radio; in magazines, comics and anthologies; and online. His latest stories are in Retro Horror, *published by Nightmare Press and available from Amazon, and the online magazine* Horla *(http://www.horla.org/shadow-by-k-j-watson-horla/). K. J. Watson's website is at https://k-j-watson.webnode.co.uk.*

7

Locked in Translation
by Steven Lombardi

Lina watched the town of Kaunas pass through the windows.

'University is to left,' grumbled Šaltkalvis, her old guide. 'House is six kilometres north.'

They drove to her off-campus housing, which looked different in the dark, more isolated. She held her body, shivering. 'Will I be okay here?'

'House is safe,' Šaltkalvis said, licking his lips.

Inside, camera-laden hallways led to more camera-laden hallways, with doors that closed and refused to open.

Pounding on the door, Lina remembered how clumsily Lithuanian translates to English. There are no articles.

The house wasn't safe... it was a *safe.*

Cameras continued to roll.

STEVEN LOMBARDI's short stories have been published recently in Theme of Absence, The Fifth Di..., *and elsewhere. You can visit him at stevenlombardi.nyc.*

8

Roommate Wanted
by Benjamin Bateman

He responds to my ad within minutes, is well-spoken and clean, offers payment upfront, the new tenant dream.

'Don't go in my room,' his single demand.

Seven nights later, he isn't around. So why can I hear footsteps? My suspicions arouse.

Turn a blind ear? Blame the old pipes? Explanations seem far-fetched, none quite suffice.

I crack open his door for a quick passing-peek.

Where is his bed? And what's with these polythene sheets? - And *holy-f...!* - there's blood on the floor, faint outlines of... feet!?

'We could've been friends,' comes his voice, sneaking up from behind, 'I wanted to *try*.'

BENJAMIN BATEMAN is an aspiring author with one complete speculative fiction novel, for which he is currently seeking representation. He has led a varied life, with accrued experience from many careers and niches. You can find him on Twitter @3enjamin3ateman.

9

Coins Collected in Jars Bought Our First Home
by Keely O'Shaughnessy

The day after we move in, I find a string of coloured pearls nestled beneath a floorboard. Like a magpie, I stow them in my dresser drawer. Braids of cable tighten around my throat.

Ripping out the kitchen, there's a brass key in the wall cavity: filigree handle, inlaid with tortoiseshell. I keep it in my coveralls and the metal takes root in my flesh.

With each new find weaved into my nest of treasures, things blur. The face in a cameo brooch laughs as I swallow it.

The stairs mumble something I can't hear, but I see their teeth.

KEELY O'SHAUGHNESSY is a fiction writer with Cerebral Palsy. She is Managing Editor at Flash Fiction Magazine. *Her short fiction has appeared in anthologies and literary magazines, and her most recent publications include* Solstice Shorts Festival 2020, 50-Word Stories *and* The Daily Drunk. *She is a 2020 Pushcart nominee. Find her on Twitter @KeelyO_writer.*

10

Sweet Dreams
by Sarah McPherson

She takes a big slice of housewarming cake.

'May I be excused?'

A hand waves. Sliding under their grown-up indifference, she flees the table for the quiet of her room; her sanctuary. Carefully, she pulls the cake into two not-quite halves, sucking icing off her fingers. The bigger piece goes on the floor on a piece of tissue. Without looking, she pushes it under the edge of the bed with her foot.

Silence. The noises won't start till all the lights are out.

By dawn the cake is gone but the girl remains, sleepless. Every morning a little paler. Hungry.

SARAH McPHERSON is a Sheffield-based writer and poet, with work published in Ellipsis Zine, Splonk, STORGY, Emerge Literary Journal, The Cabinet of Heed, *and elsewhere. She has been long/shortlisted in competitions including* Writers' HQ, Reflex Fiction *and* Cranked Anvil. *She tweets as @summer_moth and blogs at https://theleadedwindow.blogspot.com/.*

11

A Dusty Duet
by Rickey Rivers Jr.

The old house had a couple kissing within.

'It's okay,' he said. 'We're safe here.'

Regardless of reassurance, Sarah felt uneasy. Her eyes shifted to every corner she could see. The house was much too quiet.

'Marty, can we stop?'

'What's wrong?'

'This house is wrong. It freaks me out.'

'Come on, Sarah.'

A speck of dust fell from the ceiling. It landed between them.

'Only dust,' said Marty.

Sarah looked up and saw more bits of dust fall.

She stood.

Dust continued to fall, soon covering Marty. This made Sarah sneeze.

The sneeze blew half of Marty's face off.

RICKEY RIVERS JR. was born and raised in Alabama. He is a writer and cancer survivor. His work has appeared in The Gray Sisters, Back Patio Press, Hybrid Fiction *(among other publications). You can find him at storiesyoumightlike.wordpress.com. You may find something you like there. He's also on Twitter @storiesyoumight.*

12

Worms Wiggle
by Yukari Kousaka

Translated by Toshiya Kamei

'Are you all right, sis?' I glance sideways while we play a video game. 'Ever since you came home, you seem—I don't know—different.'

A few weeks ago, she went missing while traveling. Worms wiggle inside her eyes, slowly eating away their host. They too have found home.

'Lost your touch, sis? You used to beat me all the time.'

She nods, her eyes nailed to the screen.

'Who are you again?' she asks, stifling her yawn.

I frown and look her in the eye.

The worms crawl out of her eyes and fall down her cheeks like tears.

Born in Osaka in 2001, YUKARI KOUSAKA is a Japanese poet, fiction writer, and essayist. Translated by Toshiya Kamei, her short fiction has appeared in New World Writing.

13

The Snap
by Tiffany Michelle Brown

Peter stood in the dark hallway, waiting.

'You have to offer it blood or else it won't show up,' his friend Mark had said, and so Peter had pierced his ankle with a thumbtack. Blood dripped down his foot, kissing the awaiting floorboards.

Peter held his phone, the device toggled to camera mode, ready. Mark had promised him twenty bucks if he could get a picture of the demon.

Creeeeeeeeaaaaak.

Peter snapped a picture. On the screen, he stared into a maw of splintered wood lined with teeth.

Mark was wrong. It wasn't a demon.

The house was hungry.

TIFFANY MICHELLE BROWN is a California-based writer who once had a conversation with a ghost over a pumpkin beer. Her fiction has been featured by Sliced Up Press, Cemetery Gates Media, Fright Girl Winter, *and the* NoSleep Podcast.

You can find her on Twitter @tiffebrown and at tiffanymichellebrown.wordpress.com.

14

Get Out
by Joe Scipione

'Who are you?' I said, still half asleep. She stood on the other side of my bedroom, staring at me.

'I have lived here for a long time.' She floated toward me.

'What do you want?'

'I want you to leave,' she said. She stood over me. Her face was clear, her skin pale, her eyes like two black marbles.

She reached out toward me; I covered my face, but it did no good. I felt her pull me up out of bed. I was floating next to her, looking down at my empty body.

'Now get out!' She said.

JOE SCIPIONE lives in Illinois with his wife and two children. He is a senior contributor and horror book reviewer at horrorbound.net and a member of the Horror Writers Association. He can be found on Twitter or Instagram @JoeScipione0 and at joescipione.com.

15

Dare Gone Bad
by Patricia Elliott

Dark gargoyles loomed overhead, watching over the estate. Large stone lions guarded the ancient entrance. Chester froze, certain their red eyes were watching him.

He shook his head. It had to be his imagination. All he had to do was spend one night and a million dollars would be his. Swallowing hard, he took a step towards the stairs.

Someone's breath tickled the hairs on his neck. He spun around. No one was there. 'Stop being silly. Just do it!' He raced up the stairs and pushed open the door. A trapdoor released, and he plummeted to his death below.

PATRICIA ELLIOTT is a multi-published author who lives in beautiful British Columbia with her family. Now that her lovely kids are all teenagers, she has decided to actively pursue her passion for the written word—namely, anything to do with romance, horror and suspense. You can find her on Facebook as AuthorPatriciaElliott and on patriciaelliottromance.com.

16

House Addition
by K.M. Bennett

I arrived at the suburban mansion to fix a leaky water heater. Since the lady hadn't even managed to shut off the waterline, I certainly didn't expect any custom carpentry. Still, exiting the utility closet, I noticed a hollow thud underfoot. Lifting a small mat revealed a trap door and tarnished brass ring. A slim deadbolt held it down, shining like new. I opened it and a man's dark-ringed eyes blinked up at me. The clicking of heels approached from behind and a hand fell upon me. 'Oh dear. I suppose it's time to expand,' she said, pushing me down inside.

K.M. BENNETT's work has appeared in several anthologies, including the Daughters of Darkness *all-women horror anthology. Her work has also been produced on multiple podcasts, including the* NoSleep Podcast *and* ManaWaker Flash Fiction *podcast. You can learn more at ThatKatieLady.com or by following @That_Katie_Lady on Twitter.*

17

How to Build a Ghost
by Kyle Winkler

House possessed awareness of human life inside. Waiting, resisting. Learning, taxonomizing.

The parents and babies opened windows, shut doors, adjusted the chimney flue. The babies weren't gentle. They futzed with sockets, ripped carpet, scraped baseboards with nickels, quarters. House attuned to Youngest Boy because he spoke when House reached out.

'Do I know what I want?' House thought. 'Yes. I know I want.'

House communicated. Spacetime shifted in the kitchen as Youngest Boy scooted a wooden horse along the linoleum.

Zoop! Goner.

Where did the boy go? House thought.

'I'm right here!' Youngest Boy said from inside the bones of House.

KYLE WINKLER's speculative fiction has appeared in Conjunctions, The Rupture, and is forthcoming in a Scare Street *anthology. He's found online at kylewinkler.net and on Twitter @bleakhousing. He lives in NE Ohio.*

18

Open House
by Emma Kathryn

A couple stood in shock, watching as blood dripped down the walls of the den.

‘Oh, pay that no mind,’ the realtor beamed. Her smile didn’t reach her eyes. ‘That almost never happens and, when it does, there’s almost no mess.’

The couple ran. Another sale lost.

The realtor was exasperated. In the room, a shadow moved. ‘You think this is funny?’ she said to the air.

Something creaked in the darkest corner.

‘I don’t and if you think this isn’t worth the commission, you’re wrong.’

The thing growled.

‘See you tomorrow,’ she sighed and stormed off, clipboard in hand.

EMMA KATHRYN is a horror fanatic from Glasgow, Scotland. You can find her on Twitter @girlofgotham. When she's not scaring herself to death, she is one half of The Yearbook Committee Podcast *or she's streaming indie games on Twitch. She is rather tiny and rather mad.*

19

Untwinned
by Elle Jauffret

They would soon outgrow their home, he thought, as he pushed his sibling's feet away from his face. He would have to live on his own, with only his skin for protection—an upcoming reality that frightened him to his very core. Unless he remained small, hidden, like a tiny cockroach on a dark floor. Letting himself shrivel until his brother absorbed him, as planned, he ate just enough to survive as a benign tumour. Babies must leave the comfort of their mother's womb, but he could live longer, a parasite in his twin's body, hoping never to be found.

ELLE JAUFFRET is a French American writer and Californian attorney who writes across genres. You can find her at ellejauffret.com or on Twitter/Instagram @ellejauffret.

20

Autumn's Dance
by Lumen Ros

A breeze slips in through the window. Autumn memories mingle within its tepid caress.

Soon…

Crickets will serenade the full moon. Toads will sing their baritone song. Howling wolves will elevate the symphony.

I'll dance barefoot, tossing herbs and flowers into the caldron, bubbling with love's broth and a pound of aunt Carina's flesh. I'll recite ancient words. Call you forth.

You'll whisper dark promises laced in honey, tempt my heated skin with sinuous, cold fingers. In the morning, we'll have breakfast—pickled sausage from Uncle's thigh, and a warm brew of his crimson elixir.

I'll welcome you home, my love.

LUMEN ROS is the author of 'Hardingfele's Lullaby', published in The Mad River Literary Journal, and 'Mother of Darkness' in Midnight Mosaic. *Various works, short stories, and poetry, including 'Mortal Coil' and 'The Sun in Someone Else's Sky' are featured in* Lit Up *and* P.S. I Love You. *You can find her on Twitter: https://twitter.com/LumenRos_author, and Medium: https://medium.com/@lumenros.*

THERE'S NO PLACE LIKE HOME

21

Gingerbread
by Isaac Menuza

If a gingerbread man lives in a gingerbread house,

Is his home made of flesh?

When he returns from work, gumdrop briefcase in hand,

How do his children greet him?

Do they descend from bone-white eaves and sluice,

Down the treacly frosting that tacks the roof?

When the gingerbread man touches them,

Can he help but wonder

That they were made kin and not kindling?

Can they understand that, beneath the cotton snow,

And the red-dripped canes, and the cracked candy cobbles,

Lies a mille-feuille of tissue?

That the very foundation of their home

Tends the bones of the unfortunate.

ISAAC MENUZA is an author of speculative fiction and horror that probes the darkest recesses of the human condition. He lives in Washington, D.C. with his wife, three children, and whatever slimy critters his son detains for temporary imprisonment. Learn more at www.isaacmenuza.com.

22

The Metamorphouse by Jacek Wilkos

My house is constantly changing. Furniture moves, rooms transform, doors vanish, new ones appear, leading to unknown rooms through slender corridors. One day a tree grew in the middle of the living room, the next I was walking on the walls.

Only the windows disappeared permanently.

I don't know why these phenomena take place or what caused them. I haven't found any pattern. I wander in this strange building, losing track of time and sanity.

My own home terrifies me.

There's only one thing I fear more—that one day I'll find a way out and see what's happening outside.

JACEK WILKOS is an engineer from Poland. He is addicted to buying books, he loves black coffee, dark ambient music and abandoned places. He writes mostly horror drabbles. His work has been published in numerous anthologies by Black Hare Press, Alien Buddha Press, Eerie River Publishing, KJK publishing and Insignia Stories. You can find him on Facebook as Jacek.W.Wilkos.

23

Faces on the Walls
By C.M. Saunders

I see them all the time, these faces on the walls.

Every day.

Sometimes they are happy, other times they are sad. Sometimes they are familiar, other times they are strangers to me.

My new friends.

Nobody else sees them.

As a child, I remember pointing them out to my mother. She told me not to be so silly: there was nothing there.

No faces.

After that, I stopped pointing them out.

I talk to them in secret, and sometimes sing to them.

They like it.

These faces are the only things that I know will never leave me.

Never.

Christian Saunders, who writes fiction as C.M. SAUNDERS, is a freelance journalist and editor from south Wales. His work has appeared in almost 100 magazines, e-zines and anthologies worldwide including Fortean Times, The Literary Hatchet, ParABnormal, Fantastic Horror, Haunted MTL, Feverish Fiction *and* Crimson Streets, *and he has held staff positions at several leading UK magazines ranging from Staff Writer to Associate Editor. His books have been both traditionally and independently published, the latest release being* Tethered *on Terror Tract Publishing.*

You can find him at cmsaunders.wordpress.com.

24

The Old Muller Mansion
by Alanna Robertson-Webb

The ancient, gothic Muller Mansion perched on the hill above Berkley Street, curtainless windows glaring balefully down on the townsfolk who had once praised and adored it.

Each cookie-cutter condo that sprung up was another wound, another blight against the superior architecture and awe-inspiring craftsmanship of the Manor.

How could the people be so cruel?

The once-beautiful house grew furious, the spirit of each long-dead Muller lending necrotic slivers of power to the dusty halls.

Soon the house would be strong enough to unleash its pent-up wrath upon those who abandoned it, and not a soul would be left standing.

ALANNA ROBERTSON-WEBB is an author and editor who enjoys long weekends of LARPing, is terrified of sharks and finds immense fun in being the editor-in-chief at Eerie River Publishing. She one day aspires to run her own nerd-themed restaurant, as well as her own LARP game.

She has edited over ten books, such as Infected *by Blair Daniels,* A Cure for Chaos: Horror Stories from Hospitals and Psych Wards *by Haunted House Publishing,* The Deliverer *by Tara Devlin and all of the current Eerie River Publishing anthologies. Alanna's writing has been published in over seventy different collections, and her work can be found at: https://arwauthor.wixsite.com/arwauthor and at amazon.com/author/alannarobertsonwebb.*

25

Barney
by Benjamin Bateman

'Get a pet. You need reason to get out of bed in the mornings,' my therapist says, without looking up from his notepad.

That night, I adopt Barney.

He's a bit long in his remaining tooth, like me.

He prefers to stay home, locked safely away from their judgmental, gawking eyes, like me.

And most important of all, he lusts after the succulent taste of human flesh.

Like me.

Of course, being a hamster, he needs me to service his needs.

I send my therapist a thank you card and cancel next week's appointment. Barney and I have plans now.

BENJAMIN BATEMAN is an aspiring author with one complete speculative fiction novel, for which he is currently seeking representation. He has led a varied life, with accrued experience from many careers and niches. You can find him on Twitter @3enjamin3ateman.

26

Bubble Bath
by Antonia Rachel Ward

Invigorating Bath Soak. A free sample. It smelt good, so I used the lot; stepped into the foaming bubbles. I like my baths scalding, so I didn't notice the tingling sensation at first. Just lay back, letting the water cover me up to my neck. The prickles spread over my body, intensifying, turning my nerves to flame. I scrabbled to climb out. Slivers of flesh fell away from my fingers, blood coating the white enamel. They found me curled up on the mat, raw and screaming, contorted with pain as the acid sunk through my skin. It burned for hours.

ANTONIA RACHEL WARD is a writer of horror, Gothic and speculative fiction based in Cambridgeshire, UK. Her short stories have been published by Black Hare Press and Friday Flash Fiction. You can find her on Twitter @AntoniaRachelW1, Instagram @antoniarachelward or at antoniarachelward.com.

27

Burn
by Matthew McNichols

I lean over the kitchen table, my tired eyes closed, my back towards the cellar door.

I can hear it.

A suction sound, like footsteps through mud. The evil heart of the house, making its way up the stairs.

I can smell the gas from the broken oven line. I pray it's enough.

My hands shake as I open the box of matches.

The cellar door creaks open.

I turn and look.

What stands before me is worse than I could imagine. Generations of my families' sins manifested in physical form.

It reaches out.

I strike the match and hope.

MATTHEW McNICHOLS has spent over twenty years working in the printing industry, most of which was spent daydreaming about not working in the printing industry. He lives in Southern California with his wife and son.

28

Warm Thoughts
by A. Whittenberg

Can life be sustained off a windowsill's moisture, a lead pipe's sweat? Someone spills the orange juice we've been rationing. It spreads more sunshine across the room. We splinter our tongues lapping it off the wooden floor.

In the glow of night, a man bursts in and steals thirty-three ounces of water. I should have shot him, we're all going to die anyway this way.

As want drips into need, it's a good news, bad news sort of thing. My once-optimistic roommates have long since soured. They see what I've always seen. Contentment? It's all a matter of degrees.

A. WHITTENBERG is a Philadelphia native who has a global perspective. If she wasn't an author she'd be a private detective or a jazz singer. She loves reading about history and true crime. Her novels include Sweet Thang, Hollywood and Maine, Life is Fine, Tutored *and* The Sane Asylum.

29

The House Stands
by Alec Thompson

The house stands empty and bereft. Streaks of grime and negligence line its bricks and slatternly wooden planks. Even the chimney seems to slump, as though the gravity of disuse pulls it to ultimate fate.

This is the house where the family was killed. Victims of accidental happenstance, of placement, and the murderous thieves in the night. The neighbourhood children sing:

Four there,

four gone,

see the blood flow to the lawn.

There hadn't been any… suffocation was the way. Now their spirits choke the house from within, until one day the chimney will lead the collapse in upon itself.

ALEC THOMPSON lives with his family in Austin, Texas. He holds a BA in Communication Studies from Texas A&M University-Corpus Christi and studied for a MA in Radio, Television, and Film at the University of North Texas. When not writing, he works outdoors for local Parks and Recreation. Follow him on Twitter @aalecthompson.

30

Hiding Spot
by Steve Neal

Marion's parents didn't know all her hiding spots throughout the house, only some discovered after exhaustive games of hide 'n' seek. The crawlspace between floors was her favourite; well-hidden and difficult to navigate even with a child's frame.

Waking after an unintentional nap enveloped in darkness, she panicked. Sunlight no longer illuminated the dusty passage through the floorboards. Unsure which way led to the entrance hatch in the coat closet, Marion started to crawl. After a minute, a distant amber shimmer caught her eye. It darted up to her face with jagged movements.

'They'll never find you here,' it hissed.

STEVE NEAL is an English-born writer currently surviving the summers of Florida with his supportive wife and less supportive cats. As a lifelong horror fanatic, he enjoys poking at the unknown and seeing what comes crawling out, as long as it isn't spiders.

Follow him on Twitter @SteveNealWrites.

31

Listening In
by K.J. Watson

After years perched on the roof and listening to the occupants within the house, the gargoyle understood iniquity. And today, it heard each word Miss Grant's nephew uttered.

The gargoyle perceived that the nephew intended to bully and evict Miss Grant so that he could claim the property for himself. This wouldn't do.

When the nephew exited the house, the gargoyle dropped moss on him. Perplexed and angry, the nephew fetched a ladder and climbed.

The gargoyle stared stonily ahead; then it shoved the ladder.

The nephew's body sprawled on the ground. Miss Grant needn't seek another home just yet.

K. J. WATSON's fiction has appeared on the radio; in magazines, comics and anthologies; and online. His latest stories are in Retro Horror, *published by Nightmare Press and available from Amazon, and the online magazine* Horla *(http://www.horla.org/shadow-by-k-j-watson-horla/). K. J. Watson's website is at https://k-j-watson.webnode.co.uk.*

32

Uninvited
by Demi-Louise Blackburn

A fist slams against the front door. Natalie stares at the lock, reassured to see it holds strong, and her breathing slows.

I'm safe. They can't possibly get in. If they bang on the door again, I'll call the police.

Whatever is on the other side seems to hear her thoughts.

The creaking of wood follows. A thin shadow slips through the seam of the frame, lock forgotten, and Natalie's body freezes. Long fingers wave at her from the gap in the door. She retreats. It squeezes into her home. *Her* space.

The creature cocks its paper-thin skull, and grins.

DEMI-LOUISE BLACKBURN lives in a small town in West Yorkshire, England. She's found homes for some of her stories with Kandisha Press *and* All Worlds Wayfarer *and continues to chip away at a number of other projects. In her free time, she likes visiting the coast, collecting taxidermy insects, and watching documentaries.*

You can find her at demi-louise.com.

33

Waiting
by Shelby Dollar

I'm dying again in your shower,

Watching you obsess over wrinkles and weight.

You hoped butchering me was worth it,

So much blood, not much fat.

You made do,

Did the chants, struck a deal.

Boiled me into a dozen bars, my tiny coffins.

Water like acid on my body, you drag me

Across your skin, my mouth tasting filth and brine.

But I'm not done with you yet,

I'm growing in the grout, where you step gingerly.

Don't want to slip, crack yourself open,

And die.

In the shower, alone,

But you won't, I'll be there,

Waiting,

And ready.

SHELBY DOLLAR lives in Kansas City, Missouri. Her fiction can be found in Magnificent Cowlick Media's anthologies, Black Buttons Vol. 1, Vol. 3*, and* Route 666: Four on the Floor. *When she isn't writing, she spends time with her husband and Wally, their rescue dog. Visit her website at https://shelbydollar.wordpress.com/.*

34

The Home of Puppets
by Biswajit Ganguly

The Puppet House was such a haunted place that even the bravest of the brave feared to spend a night there. I challenged the local people and entered there one night. Nothing happened until I slept.

In the middle of the night, I woke up. I sensed that many amputated hands like spiders were moving around my body. I screamed and tried to break free. They held me tightly. They dragged me to a container and locked me inside.

In the morning, the local people entered the house. No, they could not find me. But they found one new puppet.

BISWAJIT GANGULY is a Bengali-language author of the science fiction novel B-3456, and humour novellas Chhataman *and* Kyabla-pur. *His poems and short stories have been published in Bengali and English magazines and anthologies. He is working on a collection of horror stories at present.*

35

The Four-Armed Man Kept Under the Steps by Patrick Barb

We kept the four-armed man under the back steps outside our house in the woods. He chipped away at the paint, scratching out flakes with his long, candle-wax-coloured nails working double-time.

We promised the four-armed man that we'd never let him go. On mischievous days, when I ran home from our backyard forest, I'd peer between splintered gaps and see his four arms reaching and his face howling with red, impotent rage.

We moved away years ago, returning to the city.

I wonder if the house is gone. And if so, what does the four-armed man do about broken promises?

PATRICK BARB is a freelance writer and editor from the southern United States, currently living (and trying not to freeze to death) in Saint Paul, Minnesota. His short horror fiction appears in Boneyard Soup Magazine *(forthcoming),* Shiver: A Chilling Horror Anthology, *and* Hookman and Friends. *For more of his work, visit patrick-barb.com and follow him on Twitter @pbarb.*

36

Buzz
by Gus Wood

Harold shot awake like a middle-aged bullet. It was quiet outside. The TV was off. Nothing explained the low, forceful buzzing sound he heard.

Awake, he waited in bed for the doctor's office to open.

They talked about tinnitus, about TMJ, about tumors. 'How 'bout a scan?'

The MRI almost drowned out the buzzing. For a moment.

Then Harold heard the ripping cocoon, the wings, the hundred blooming legs bursting free from their outgrown home in his now bleeding ear.

He wouldn't live to hear the swarm find the doctor. The wet sound of new eggs finding a home.

GUS WOOD is a game designer and horror movie critic. You can find his work at https://gusfuss.itch.io/ (Games) and https://gusonhorror.myportfolio.com/ (movie writing). He hopes you read this by candlelight.

37

Of Kitchen Revolutions and the Unappreciated Anima of Appliances
or
The Revolution
by Alec Thompson

The Addisons came home to utter confusion. Front door battered out, glass broken on the floors, pictures canted or lying where they fell. The parents shielded their children from entry.

'Just, what in the…'

Dad moved in, sidestepped pebbled glass and splinters. Surveyed the chaos, the detritus, the sense of unbridled revelry. Then he walked into the kitchen and caught them.

'What—'

He watched the gadgetry in pandemonium. The blender masticating trash, the oven laughing charred oven mitts, the fridge spewing rancid groceries. Upon seeing him the appliances ceased, became lifeless.

But all was clear; there had been a revolution.

ALEC THOMPSON lives with his family in Austin, Texas. He holds a BA in Communication Studies from Texas A&M University-Corpus Christi and studied for a MA in Radio, Television, and Film at the University of North Texas. When not writing, he works outdoors for local Parks and Recreation. Follow him on Twitter @aalecthompson.

38

The Basement
by Shannon Walker

After Mom died, my Dad had reoccurring dreams where she would laugh at him from the basement. Night after night, her voice urged him to the door but every time he reached for the knob, he awoke.

One morning Dad called me. Inconsolable, he said the door opened, but the basement was empty. Days later he died in his sleep.

That night, Mom's laughter filled my dreams.

Unable to resist her voice, I followed. The door opened and, desperate to see her, it was only halfway down the stairs when I noticed Dad's handwriting scrawled across the floor.

'Don't look up.'

SHANNON WALKER is a hobbyist writer and aspiring author who has travelled North America with her husband in their big red van named Clifford. She currently lives in British Columbia where she lives without Wi-Fi for seven months out of the year working in the backcountry. You can find her at swalkerwrites.ca.

39

The House Calls You
by Wolf Weston

One day you reached for your phone, and it reached back. Squirming appendages shot out around the squares of your apps and wrapped themselves around your wrists, swirling up your elbow and your collarbone, wringing their cords around your neck. Before you could stop them, you had given an arm. Your stolen hand lifted the phone to your ear, and more cord bound it fast to your head. A strand crawled into your canal, past the drum and tapped your brain. The trickling sound of you losing yourself. The voice was hissing: *We're the only ones that can love you.*

WOLF WESTON is a musician and burgeoning speculative fiction writer whose performances have gained attention from major publications such as Pitchfork, The New York Times, Impose Magazine, and more. Wolf resides in Brooklyn, NY, minding her business and feeding her cat, Crow.

40

Fleeing the Nest
by Abi Marie Palmer

Here's how you escape the family:

Wait until they sleep. Extricate yourself carefully—carefully!—from their nest. Don't. Wake. Arachnia. She is not kind to deserters.

Creep barefoot to the old lift shaft. The webs will snare you. Free yourself using your teeth—sharpen them on a rock before you go. Scramble silently, frantically, up the narrow shaft.

The light above ground will burn your eyes. Ignore the pain and run. Arachnia's children will soon follow.

Return to the home you left behind. Apologise for running away. Try to forget what you have seen. Slowly, learn to be human again.

ABI MARIE PALMER is a writer and English teacher from the UK. Her work has appeared in Pulp Modern Flash, Nymphs and Black Hare Press publications. You can find her flash fiction on Instagram @lightningfiction and her other work at abimariepalmer.com

HOME SWEET HOME

41

Undream
by Madison LaTurner

When he comes home—because he always does—he brings me flowers, and life is perfect. It goes like this: We eat dinner together every night because we are together. Our daughter tells us the kinds of things that regular children would. My husband and I smile at each other proudly. When I reach for his hand, his skin is there. When I hug him, his body is warm. We laugh because we are happy. We smile because we have things to smile about. Everything is perfect and normal and lovely. This is real. This is happening. This is real.

MADISON LATURNER is a writer from Salt Lake City, Utah, and absolutely believes they were a boat in a past life. Their work has appeared in Rune Bear Weekly, *and you can find them on Twitter @maddylaturner.*

42

Home is Where the Body Lies
by John Lane

Ever since I was interred three months ago, I feel right at home.

In fact, I get along great with the neighbours.

To my left, George Sandhoe reminisces about how a percussion cap rifle made him the first casualty on the Gettysburg battlefield.

To my right, Mary Longenecker shares about her time teaching the ABC's to the children of Stevens Elementary School.

George and Mary never ask about my three pack a day habit.

We carry on to the wee hours of the morning.

Some passers-by complain about the quiet, but they're dead wrong.

We talk.

They're just not listening.

JOHN LANE's stories and essays have appeared in Rejected Manuscripts, Dark Dossier Magazine, Trembling with Fear, The Drabble, Pure Slush, Morbidly Beautiful, Celestial Toyroom *and other venues.*

John's story, 'Dimension Traveler,' made the top of Rejected Manuscripts*' 'Most Read' list and was voted on their 'Current Top Ten' list.*

43

A Home Cooked Meal
by Violet James

Incantations swirl. Quiet as a whisper. Deadly as a snake. He will suffer for his transgressions.

The fire crackles and the embers glow beneath the caldron. Smoke fills my lungs, but no matter—soon he will taste the bile of my vengeance. Soon the spell will be cast. A smile creases my cheek. I will coddle him, and kiss his pouty lips while the blood of betrayal trickles from his veins.

I stir the pot, and pull from it the secret ingredient. Stricken, he gasps. His lover's face stares back at him. She is a touch wrinkled, soaking in brine.

VIOLET JAMES is a compulsive writer. Whenever she has a free moment, she is at the computer either writing or editing her novel. She loves to craft words into a scene sumptuous for the mind as well as the eyes. Horror has captured her imagination, especially when it is linked with romance.

You can find her on Twitter @VioletJames21and Medium @violetjames51.

44

Topsy-Turvy Man
by Antonia Rachel Ward

'Topsy-Turvy Man comes from Topsy-Turvy Land,
He wears gloves on his feet and shoes on his hands.
He has hair on his knees and a sock on his head,
He eats rats for dinner and sleeps under the bed.'

'That's a clever poem,' I said, tucking my son in. 'I hope you're not worried about him sleeping under your bed.'

Charlie shook his head, but his eyes were frightened. To reassure him, I checked the shadows under his bed.

'See? Nothing.'

But as I switched out the light Charlie whispered:

'He's not under *my* bed. He's under *yours.*'

ANTONIA RACHEL WARD is a writer of horror, Gothic and speculative fiction based in Cambridgeshire, UK. Her short stories have been published by Black Hare Press and Friday Flash Fiction. You can find her on Twitter @AntoniaRachelW1, Instagram @antoniarachelward or at antoniarachelward.com. Topsy-Turvy Man is her daughter's imaginary friend.

45

Dead Man's Chair
by J.M. Faulkner

Sit in grandad's chair, and he'll whisper things to you. My brother's words buzz behind my clenched eyes. *Dead things.*

Leave him a beer, and he'll drink it for you.

The handcrafted, antique rocking chair sits in the parlour, ready to creak floorboards. I shake my head and exhale. He's pulling my leg, I think, but I've already got a beer in my hand.

I place it beside the chair. The arms are darker than the body, oiled by weathered hands.

Backing away, I make a swift exit. I'm at the door when I hear it—the chair pitching forwards.

J.M. FAULKNER is a British English teacher living in Prague, Czech Republic. It is the perfect place for him to steep himself in the architecture and tumultuous history that fuels his curiosity. Outside of work, you can find him hiking in splendid, Bohemian forests with his beagle. You can find him at jmfaulkner.com.

46

My Brother Will Save Me
by Gordon Dunleavy

Home is where the heart is, but it's also where the monsters are. They live in the basement… during the day. But at night, when sleep is but a few long blinks away, they climb those creaky steps and come up to play.

Their snarls break the quiet. Nobody in the house can hear them, only me. This is my own personal hell.

They're close.

From beneath my brother's bed, I wait as their drool slaps the hollow floor.

My brother will help me. Not to fight for my life, but to fill their bellies so I won't have to.

GORDON DUNLEAVY has been published by Scare Street, Eerie River Publishing, and Other Worldly Women Press. His story for Scare Street was part of an Amazon number one selling anthology. It's on Audible and being translated into two other languages. Gordon is finishing up his latest novel. You can find him at GordonDunleavy.com.

47

Amongus
by Kathleen Allen

I am having trouble breathing.

The advice: 'Check for mould.'

No mould, but mushrooms grow in the bathroom vent, bloated and sanguine, pulsing like a heaving bosom. They explode into wet, jellied fragments like clotted blood when touched. I pull apart the pipes to save my home.

The house sags, sodden and red as wine in the corners. I touch a wall and it rips apart like wet cardboard. Behind the walls sprouts carmine rot. I lay my head down on my pillow at night and it comes away dripping. My pillow and my dreams are made of crimson decay.

KATHLEEN ALLEN is a writer of speculative fiction located in the Pacific Northwest, home of dark winters, excellent coffee, and myriad unknown cryptids. She lives in pleasant harmony with her family and the unseen lurkers in the crawlspace. Kathleen's short fiction has been previously published by Madness Heart Press.

48

Anglerfish
by Corey Farrenkopf

There is a candle in a window. Another in the hall, in a side room. A fourth burns in the closet. A fifth illuminates the narrow attic.

You climb over rafters, hoping to pinch each wick before the house catches. You hear the flick of a lighter. The next candle visibly flares beneath an air vent. Retrace your steps and blow out the candle before the carpet catches.

The lighter flick reverberates in the next room.

Another candle.

Another lunge.

Another breath.

You never see the one who lights the flame, but you never run out of candles to snuff.

COREY FARRENKOPF's short stories have been published in or are forthcoming from Tiny Nightmares, Bourbon Penn, The Southwest Review, Catapult, Wigleaf, Flash Fiction Online, Campfire Macabre, *and elsewhere. He is currently working on a novel with his agent Marie Lamba of the Jennifer DeChiara Literary Agency. He is also the Fiction Editor for the* Cape Cod Poetry Review. *For more information, visit his website at* coreyfarrenkopf.com.

49

Construction
by Ashley Van Elswyk

A home is built of many parts.

Voices echo through the air, settling with the dust into tiny cracks in the walls. Murmurs and screams infuse the bones under a skin of prettily painted laughter, trimmed with mourning.

And touch. Curled around the doorframe, down the bannister, brushing over window sills. Gripping door knobs, against the wall, tip-toe stomping across every floorboard. Beaten, caressed.

Enduring in silence, ever-hungry for more.

Clothes, toys, hair, tears, sweat, spit, blood, breath. All leave permanent stains, traces of the living and the dead within its walls.

Any home is, by nature, a haunted one.

ASHLEY VAN ELSWYK is a queer Canadian writer of speculative fiction and poetry. When not writing, she seeks out inspiration while improving her photography on nature walks. Her work appears or is forthcoming in Green Ink Poetry *and* From the Farther Trees. *She can be found on twitter @ashvanewrites.*

50

Ms. Wail's Home for Boys
by Tonia Markou

Jonesy follows Ms. Wail to the basement. I tiptoe after them.

'She's…in here?'

His aunt from Australia is supposed to come for him.

'Go on.'

When Jonesy hesitates, Ms. Wail shoves him inside the storage room. Silver glistens in her grip.

'No!' I lunge forward, but she swats me away like a fly.

With one quick stroke she cuts his throat. Blood gushes out of him, reminding me of the fountain behind my childhood home.

My fingers trace a scar reaching from ear to ear. The memories flood back in.

I've been in this room before. We all have.

TONIA MARKOU is a Greek-German polyglot and globetrotter with an unhealthy obsession for stationery, mugs, pyjamas and Chuck Taylors. Her short fiction has appeared in Havok, Corvid Queen, little somethings press, Scarlet Leaf Review *and other journals. You can follow her on Twitter, Facebook and Medium at @toniawrites.*

51

Communion
by Benjamin Gardner

I looked up to see the stars; I had somehow fallen asleep in the basement.

I must have been woken by the noise of our first house being ripped in half and broken like bread.

Now I could hear my breathing, but nothing else. I looked at the two floors above me with furniture piled in corners and walls resting at strange angles. The darkness moved, tentacles of shadows creeping around everything we owned. As the serpentine arms reached down into the basement, I scrambled up the stairs and climbed over debris, running out into the street in my nightclothes.

BENJAMIN GARDNER is a writer, artist, and professor living in the Midwestern United States. His writing has recently been included in Mysterium Tremendum #1 *and* Night Terrors Vol. 4.

52

Janet
by Alexis DuBon

Janet liked to play with dolls,
She liked to play with toys,
Preferring her ceramic friends
To living girls and boys.

Her parents always wanted her
To go outside and play,
But in her room inside her home,
Was where she'd rather stay.

Finally they had enough,
And forced the girl outside,
But the moment that they did,
Janet abruptly died.

She had given to her dolls
Not just a gift, a toll;
Donating to each
A little sliver of her soul.

Regrettably, without her friends,

No longer safely home,

Janet was no more

Than rotten meat on hollow bone.

ALEXIS DUBON spent most of her life waiting tables until quarantine, when, removed from all the real people out in the world, she decided to make up some new ones to keep her company. She lives in New York with her dog Schatzi.

53

Nobody Cared
by Petina Strohmer

Home was a place where you could...

lie, steal, cheat, fight, shout, swear, live on takeaways, drink, smoke, take drugs, have sex, lie in, play truant, stay out or have loud, all-night parties with friends and smash the place up.

A place where you could do anything—because nobody cared.

Home was a place where you could...

cry, scream, bleed, puke, go without proper meals or clean clothes, be lonely, afraid, ignored, forgotten, get threatened, bullied, beaten up, abused and then deal with the aftermath of abortion alone.

A place where anything could be done to you—because nobody cared.

Originally from London, PETINA STROHMER now lives in Wales. Her first novel, Truly Blue; A Rock & Roll Parable*, was published by Leaf Books in March 2009. Her second novel,* Entertaining Angels, *was published by Cinnamon Press in May 2016. She also writes short stories, plays and magazine articles.*

For more information, go to petinastrohmer.com.

54

Lazy Sundays
by Caitlin Marceau

The covers are warm. If it wasn't for the alarm ringing on the nightstand, he would stay in bed all day. He stretches, the silk pyjamas soft against his skin.

He tries to navigate the empty house from memory. It's big, expensive, and not quite to his taste, but that's okay. It's the people he stays for. He showers and tries to find something comfortable to wear. It's too tight, but will do.

He then carries the plastic tub into the kitchen, supplies prepped, before checking his borrowed watch.

The couple will be home soon, and then his fun begins.

CAITLIN MARCEAU is an author and professional editor living and working in Montreal. She holds a B.A. in Creative Writing and is a member of the Horror Writers Association. If she's not covered in ink or wading through stacks of paper, you can find her ranting about issues in pop culture or nerding out over a good book. For more, check out caitlinmarceau.ca.

55

Sleep My Sweet
by Taylor DePrince

'Mummy, mummy!' The words pull her out of her sleep. She staggers to her daughter's room; her eyes not yet accustomed to the dark. Stumbling as she enters, she can just make out her daughter in bed, guarded by stuffed animals, the blankets pulled up and her hair hanging over her face. She gets into the bed and holds her daughter, stroking her hair and reassuring her that it was only a nightmare.

Her sleepiness suddenly turns to terror as she remembers that her daughter is at her grandmother's house tonight. A low, malevolent laugh comes from under the blankets.

TAYLOR DEPRINCE is a newbie to the whole being a writer thing, so most of her work can be found on her laptop or rattling around her head. She has had poetry published in the Together poetry anthology and she currently assists with poetry workshops for a community arts organisation.

56

Ding-Dong
by Fusako Ohki

Translated by Toshiya Kamei

Ding-dong. The doorbell rings. Who can that be? I sit up in bed by reflex and rub my gummy eyes. I'm not expecting anybody. Not at this hour. I roll out of bed, go to the door, and take a peek out the peephole. Nobody's there. I click my tongue and go back to my bedroom. *Ding-dong*. What the heck? I go back out, but nobody's there. *Ding-dong*. Again? I fling the door open and yell into the darkness: 'What do you want?' I shrug and lock the door. When I slip under the covers, something cold grabs my foot.

FUSAKO OHKI is a Japanese writer from Tokyo. She obtained her master's degree in Japanese literature from Hosei University. Her debut collection of short fiction is forthcoming in 2021.

57

Little Sister Does the Dishes
by Mary Daurio

The backdoor latch sprang open, startling little sister. 'That you Momma?'

He entered the kitchen, thrusting her firmly against the counter, eyeing her budding breasts. His eager fingers feathered her soft, silky skin.

Staring straight ahead, she bit her lip, tasted blood. 'Please, no.'

Under her dress, he ripped panties, entering her softness. Harder than he'd ever been, taking his pleasure, oblivious. Her hand spidered the counter. Fingers fastened around a fork's shaft. With a plunge, she drove sharp tangs into his eye. He sagged limp, backing away bare buttocked, a howling tomcat, as the backdoor latch sprang open.

MARY DAURIO is a grandmother who likes to fiddle with words. Presently she is working on a short story compilation about her experiences as a Standardbred racehorse driver and attending Brock University, taking Creative writing. Her work has appeared online and in print.

58

Salem Village
by E.C. Hanson

My eyes locked on the flickering candle. Father's brutish ways and mother's quest to become the perfect Puritan punctured my young soul. Their resistance to a new manner of life made them expendable. I dreamed of a multitude of ploys to send them from this earth. Fortunately for them, these manifestations occurred solely within my head. But hope was restored when a group of teenage girls in Salem Village acted as if they were under the devil's spell. Their hysteria gave me a delicious idea: I contorted my slender frame, screamed to the heavens, and accused my parents of witchcraft.

E.C. HANSON is a published playwright and Horror Writers Association member. A graduate of NYU, his work has been published by Smith & Kraus and Applause Books in 8 play anthologies. More than 35 of his plays have been developed and produced across the United States. His story, 'The Roost', will be published by Collective Tales in the fall of 2021. His story, 'Taunt That Witch', will be published online by Parliament Press during their upcoming Holiday Hearth Story Event.

59

The Gifts
by Sean Ferrell

She placed the bowl of peanuts on the wall and waited. Old Elisabeth next door had taught her this five years ago.

'Give food, they bring gifts,' Old Elisabeth had said. She and Elisabeth had gifted to the crows and been gifted in return: pennies, screws, and even a ring that Elisabeth wore on her bony finger.

She invited Elisabeth to join, but heard no response to her calls. Alone, she waited. A crow came at last. It ate, flew, and returned—a glinting in its beak. She waited to collect it. It left a ring, still on one bony finger.

*SEAN FERRELL has published novels (*Man in the Empty Suit *and* NUMB*) and picture books (*I Don't Like Koala *and* The Snurtch*). He lives and works in Brooklyn, NY. He writes stories about children and adults who don't understand why they keep getting into trouble. Sometimes those stories are for adults. Sometimes for children. His work is usually speculative in nature.*

60

What Moves in the Night
by Amanda Crum

The foundation creaks with every step, a reminder of how much living has been done here.

It's pale in the sunlight, innocuous. When night hushes against the walls, I press my tongue to the roof of my mouth just to feel something solid. A tether to the world.

I cry out for my mother as heavy treads fall in the attic, a reminder that the demons still live here. They'll never leave now. I've made it too easy for them to stay. They whisper of flesh, blood, sacrifice, of dead gods.

My body is my home, and it is haunted.

AMANDA CRUM is a writer from Kentucky whose work has been published in Barren Magazine, Eastern Iowa Review, *and others. She is the author of* Tall Grass, *which is an Indie Horror Book Award nominee.*

HOME IS WHERE THE HEART IS

61

Where Your Heart Is
by Emma K. Leadley

You once told me you'd give me your heart, and I had no cause to doubt you. But, you left me.

Don't worry though, my love, I'm happy now.

Remember us sitting in front of the hearth, fire-gazing and sharing soft words? I built us a shrine there, up on the mantelpiece. There's a lock of your hair and small trinkets we shared, back when we were lovers.

And at the centre is, my love, a jar. It glows ruby red in candlelight, filled with the heart I tore from your stilling body.

I'm home. It's where your heart is.

EMMA K. LEADLEY is a UK-based writer, blogger and creative geek. She began writing as an outlet for her busy brain, and quickly realised scrawling words on a page is wired into her DNA. She's been published by multiple independent presses in the SFF and horror genres. Visit her online at https://www.autoerraticism.com/category/publications/ or on Twitter @autoerraticism.

62

Are You Watching?
by Collin Yeoh

Watch me laugh. Watch her laugh back. Watch my lips as I sip wine and watch her stare at them. Watch me scooch forward, watch our faces close enough to kiss, and watch her take up my offer. Watch her hands ride up my skirt and over the scars you gave me. Watch us make love in our bed, your bed.

Watch me come like you never made me and watch me please her like I never did you.

I'm free of you now. I killed you in this house, and now it's my house.

Now stay. And watch. Forever.

COLLIN YEOH spent a decade and a half writing advertising copy. He is now glad to spend his time writing things that won't be subject to notes like 'needs more branding'. He lives in Bangkok, Thailand and misses Malaysian food.

63

Roses for You
by Nicola Kapron

'Bury me in the garden,' you said, and I obliged. I bought so many beautiful rose bushes and arranged them just right. Now you live outside the front door, petals in your mouth. Thorns through your tongue. Roots sunk deep into your skull. You've never been more beautiful. I push through the vines and kiss you every morning before I leave for work.

'Sarah,' you moan, throat thick with leaves, 'it hurts.'

'I know,' I soothe.

'I'm not—dead—' You cough up bloodied flowers.

Another kiss. I can taste the roses. 'It's never too early to make things perfect.'

NICOLA KAPRON has previously been published by Portal Magazine, Neo-opsis Science Fiction Magazine*, and in anthologies from* Nocturnal Sirens Publishing, Rebel Mountain Press, Soteira Press, All Worlds Wayfarer*, and* Mannison Press. *Nicola lives in Nanaimo, British Columbia, with a hoard of books—mostly fantasy and horror—and an extremely fluffy cat.*

64

The Dining Room is for Decorative Purposes Only
by Tyler Norton

Mom never lets me have friends over for dinner. I don't ask, because I know the answer: The dining room is for decorative purposes only.

We eat in the kitchen, and if I peek in the dining room, Mom gets mad. She says the China hutch and chandelier are fragile. 'Just leave it alone, Josh.'

'Sorry, Mom. Won't do it again,' I lie.

It's okay, because she's lying, too. She's always staring, so I know she sees them. Dad and Erin sit at the table all the time, and they don't look like they've been in an accident at all.

TYLER NORTON is a dark fiction writer from Upstate New York. His story, 'Scenes from a Modern Yearbook', has appeared in Flash Fiction Magazine. *You can follow him on Twitter @tywritesthings or on Instagram @tylerwritesthings.*

65

Attached
by Zoe DeVoe

I love her dearly. We spend every day together, cosied up in the manor. I've never been happier with anyone else, and I've lived through many unhappy relationships. My favourite thing for her to do is to feed me. She always gives me the most delicious, home-cooked meals with the best meat. We're going to have children soon, and I could not be more pleased. I've been waiting to find someone worthy of my offspring. Unfortunately, she won't be around for their birth. It's no good being a parasite, but this is what happens when people move into my house.

ZOE DEVOE is an LGBTQ+ author with a passion for experimental horror stories. She also enjoys writing poetry. Her website can be found here: zoedevoe.com.

66

Mother's Room
by Benjamin Bateman

‘Smile! This'll be fun!’ she tells me, as the psychic arrives.

My nerves unjangle at the scent of fresh-burnt sage. Overpriced hack.

‘The energies downstairs seem clear to me. Mind if I take a look upstairs?’

‘Yes, Malcolm, your Mother's old room! If that ghost is hiding anywhere, I'll bet it's in there!’

My reluctance is ill-fated.

‘Oh, wow, yes! I'm channelling something... Mary? Your Mother's name was Mary?’

‘Marie, actually.’

‘Mary is close! Don't be grumpy! What is Marie saying?’

‘She says... she hopes the life insurance was worth it, Malcolm.’

Now I have three ghosts to deal with.

BENJAMIN BATEMAN is an aspiring author with one complete speculative fiction novel, for which he is currently seeking representation. He has led a varied life, with accrued experience from many careers and niches. You can find him on Twitter @3enjamin3ateman.

67

Where the Heart Is
by Varian Ross

Where the dead heart lies, it
haunts. Faintly your screams
echo through the rain, pelting like
razors against my widows.
Ending you was easy, now lurking
terror sets in. I fear you are lingering
here still. Shall my wait for freedom be
endless? Shall I never, ever
escape your words, the knives without steel? Is the
attic the only place safe from you, this suffocating
room where mothballs hold on to the past?
This is where I shall lay my guilty bones;
inside the attic, this graveyard of memories
shall I sleep until they find me, my heart here forever.

VARIAN ROSS is an author of queer horror fiction and poetry. 'Where the Heart Is' is an acrostic poem inspired by Poe, one of Varian's major horror influences. It is also his first published poem. Varian lives in the Midwestern United States with his family, many knitting projects, and dogs.

Varian's Twitter: https://twitter.com/VarianRoss

Varian's Website: https://varianross.com/

68

Home Blue Home
by Emilian Wojnowski

In my left hand I'm holding a photo of me and my husband Rogelio. We're young, blonde, and tanned as usual.

Rog was a fisherman whose second home was the sea. But he didn't love it more than me.

In my right hand I'm holding a piece of paper with scribble on it.

'*Her skin was pale and smooth, so was her hair, but red. So gorgeous she was, I couldn't sail hom—*'

Rogelio's last words. The last proof of his love to me and of a human's inability to resist seductive magic. And the only description of a mermaid.

To my friends who live by the Baltic Sea

EMILIAN WOJNOWSKI comes from another planet, which is why he feels bad on Earth. A philologist and translator by education, a hobbit by nature and appearance, he is constantly looking for peace, lost time, and books. Find him in such literary places as Intrinsick, Curiosities, Amon Hen, Crimeucopia *and Graham Masterton's official website.*

69

With the Angels
by Maribel Quijano

She stands over the basinet, bathed in moonlight, and gazes upon her baby's dreaming face. Closing her eyes, she inhales the intoxicating sweet scent emanating from his downy little crown. As if sensing her presence, her baby stirs, but settles—so trustful—and smiles, a sweet, carefree smile. What do people say about babies smiling in their sleep? Ah, yes, that they are in the presence of angels. The thought of her baby being with angels fills her heart with joy. She thrusts the pillow clutched to her chest over his cheeky face, and presses down, while singing a lullaby.

MARIBEL QUIJANO is a writer who lives in Australia with her husband, two children, dog and cat. When she is not writing, she likes going hiking and exploring the wonderful Australian bush. She speaks three languages, has travelled to Europe and Asia and grew up in a haunted house.

70

A Soft Heart
by Kati Lokadottir

Coming to my senses, I spat out a tooth; the second one this week. Gathering my clothes, I got dressed; Abby can't see me like this. I was still sore; he said if I didn't open my legs he would do Abby… so I did. Again.

I couldn't do this anymore. I fetched the knife to slit my veins, but then a new thought occurred to me. There were better things I could do with it.

He snored in alcohol induced stupor in his bed.

"For Abby!" I struck, and laughed.

Turns out he had a soft heart after all.

KATI LOKADOTTIR is your weird girl next door. She reads tarot, writes posthumous fiction and learns throat singing inspired by The Hu. Until very recently she wrote exclusively for her drawer. Even she doesn't know what's next, so keep an eye out for her! Write her at katilokadottir@gmail.com or visit https://www.facebook.com/katilokadottir.

71

Home Is Where the Heart Is
by Lilly Tupa

Enter slow and walk on eggshells coming through the empty halls
You will hear the curdled screaming echoed through the hallowed walls

You can try to dodge the dripping blood coming from above
But they painted the beige walls crimson for you in a twisted act of love

There is nowhere to hide in the darkened corners or the shadows
For there lie all the skeletons of which you previously tried to dispose

With all the voices in your head you'll never be alone
They say home is where the heart is
But your beating heart's stuck in this home

LILLY TUPA is a young poet who has used writing to get her through this past year. She is interested in a great many things outside of writing, none of which make her sound any less nerdy which include knitting, crocheting, reading, and buying books. Yes, she believes that reading books and buying books are two entirely different hobbies.

72

After the Honeymoon
by Electra Rhodes

'Darling, look at this.'

Alice was holding a poppet, button eyes, wearing a threadbare dress. There were pins in the bodice and a handkerchief shawl, the letters 'AB' printed in the corner.

'It was behind the panelling. In our bedroom.'

'She's rather fun,' I said, 'Shall I put her on the mantelpiece?'

The next day one of our new neighbours dropped by. He blanched when he saw the little doll.

'Oh, that's just superstition,' Alice scoffed, looking quickly away.

But she burned it that afternoon, and insisted we pack up and leave immediately.

I'll try under the floorboards next time.

E. E. RHODES is an archaeologist who accidentally lives in a castle in England. Her work can be read in numerous anthologies, journals and competition placings.

73

The Storm Door Score
by Michael Colbert

The ghost knows the storm door

Slams it open shut open

Shut when he hears us in the bedroom, twin

Beds slid together, house staff never intended

To look twice at each other, too busy wiping

Drool from orphan toddlers to relish sincere

Laughs, the collection

Of *Advocate* on the dresser.

But here we are

Another night,

Shunning poltergeists in favour

Of poppers and romping.

The gays in the attic, tucking

into each other.

The slamming's not so bad. Our first

Time, I gripped the iron headboard.

My fist could not quiet the moans as well

As this lonely ghost.

MICHAEL COLBERT loves coffee (his favourites are Costa Rican and Ethiopian) and horror films (his favourites are Candyman *and* Silence of the Lambs*). He is currently an MFA candidate in fiction at UNC Wilmington, and his writing appears or is forthcoming in* Gulf Coast, Barrelhouse*, and* Atlas Obscura*. You can find him at michael-jcolbert.com.*

74

The Sensual Spirit
by Laura Shenton

I need to run my fingers through the softness of your hair. I want to inhale deeply and take in everything about your scent as I rest my nose on your head, holding you close to me.

Wrapped around you. Your entire frame in my strength. Holding you tightly, so tightly.

All the while, being with you, as you sit in your home, blissfully unaware of my soul having dwelled here for hundreds of years.

You might sense a whisper from time to time. Or maybe a breeze that makes you shudder. You'll never see me though. You'll never know.

The format of the Hundred Word Horror anthology speaks to LAURA SHENTON in a big way as someone who is a huge fan of Edgar Allan Poe. She will be self-publishing some gothic horror novellas soon and is also a traditionally published author of several music non-fiction books. You can find her at https://www.amazon.co.uk/s?k=Laura+Shenton

75

Home Is Where the Heart Is
by Alexis DuBon

They say home is where the heart is, and for me it's true. I'm at home inside of you. No signs of forced entry, no alarms sounding. I just make myself comfortable and settle in. Undetected intruder. Until I've turned my palace to rubble and it's far too late.

Silently burrowing through ventricles and arteries, snacking and munching and grazing and feasting, I'm such a quiet houseguest, by the time you realise I'm here and try to evict me, I've already established squatting rights. By the time you realise I'm here, it's far too late.

This is my home now.

ALEXIS DUBON spent most of her life waiting tables until quarantine, when, removed from all the real people out in the world, she decided to make up some new ones to keep her company. She lives in New York with her dog Schatzi.

76

Mobile Home
by Elle Jauffret

'Where's home?'

She cringed at the question.

Born a military kid, then an enlisted Marine, her home has been military bases and duty stations. Uprooted yearly, moving boxes, quick friendships, and teary goodbyes had been her life's only constant. Until she met him—her anchor, her foundation. A man whose strong embrace and scent were the walls of her dream house. A steady shelter from the warring world in which they were pawns. An address with a beating heart.

'Home?' The chaplain repeated, handing her the triangularly folded flag and dog tags.

'You've blessed his coffin and buried him underground.'

ELLE JAUFFRET is a French American writer and Californian attorney who writes across genres. You can find her at ellejauffret.com or on Instagram @ellejauffret.

77

Home Is
by Georgia Cook

Everyone in town knew she was a witch. Nevermind her age. Nevermind her beauty. She fooled no one.

She had a cabinet, they said. Painted red. Bolted to the chimney wall.

When at last they ransacked the place, the cabinet was torn from the wall and thrown open. Inside, they found a perfectly preserved human heart, pinned through with cobblers' nails.

They buried it in the garden, burned the cabinet as well, and nobody wished to know to whom the heart belonged.

Or why, years after, a soft throbbing sound could be heard among the ruins of the old cottage.

GEORGIA COOK is an illustrator and writer from London. She has been shortlisted for the Bridport Prize, Staunch Book Prize and Reflex Fiction Award, among others, and published as both an author and reviewer. She can be found on Twitter at @georgiacooked and on her website at georgiacookwriter.com.

78

A Husband's Return
by Toshiya Kamei

'You're home early, otonosama.' Shizuka bowed, her kimono rustling. Her warrior husband stood in the gloom and stared at nothing. 'When did you get back?' His armour looked frayed and rusted. Shizuka gasped at his chalk-white face.

He stepped outside. The hens shrieked, frantically flapping their wings. Shizuka grabbed a lantern and chased him into the yard. The dim light revealed a pool of blood beside the chicken coop. Shizuka hoped against hope that a famished fox was the culprit of the mess. Then lightning flashed, illuminating her husband's deathly figure. Blood gushed from a gaping hole in his chest.

TOSHIYA KAMEI's short fiction has appeared in New World Writing.

79

My Haunted Heart
by Serena Jayne

Ghosts of my possible pasts and unfortunate futures crammed every corner and crevice of the halfway house. The haunting harmony of addiction incited an incessant itch.

One day, another apparition appeared. Not a manifestation invoked by a muddy memory or my next bad decision, rather the spectre of a previous tenant. She bared her rotted teeth as though I were covetous of her rig and tragic magic.

She stalked my every move, doing a severed marionette dance in my dreams. I gave that shattered soul a home in my heart. Embracing all her broken parts created compassion for my own.

SERENA JAYNE received her MFA in Writing Popular Fiction from Seton Hill University. When she isn't trolling art museums for works that move her, she enjoys writing in multiple fiction genres. Her short fiction has appeared in The Arcanist, Space and Time Magazine, Switchblade Magazine, *and other publications.*

You can find her at serenajayne.com and on Twitter @sj_writer.

80

Emergence
by Blaise Langlois

In the depths of darkens it sits, brooding, changing with time. It is not blind, but rather its vision lies in wait for a time when it is necessary. It is comfortable, moving with the rhythm, the cadence of her heart. Moments pass without recognition, without any significance to mark them and hide them away within. Its ancient memories awake and remind it of an oath taken. Pressure builds and it is aware that the time is nigh. Washed in warmth it is reluctant, but the call ignites an archaic fire of instinct. The calcified cage erupts, bringing it forth.

Emerging author BLAISE LANGLOIS will never turn down the chance to tell a creepy story around the campfire. She has a penchant for horror, sci-fi and dystopia with published short fiction through Eerie River Publishing, Pulp Factory E-zine and Black Hare Press. You can learn more by visiting www.ravenfictionca.wordpress.com.

HOME AT LAST

81

Back Home
by Blen Mesfin

A feeling of nostalgia washes over me as I run my hand through the torn walls of my childhood home. Its once spotless form was now layered with grime. I'd forgotten what it felt like to be here.

It was horrible.

Dysfunctional parents and a sad excuse for a brother were enough to drive you mad. Yet, now, it was almost… peaceful. Maybe it was because I could no longer hear my parents' arguing. Maybe it was that my brother was no longer here to taunt me.

Or maybe it was the metallic smell of blood stemming from their corpses.

BLEN MESFIN lives in Ethiopia with her family. When she's not writing, you will more often than not find her nose stuck in the closest book. Writing is a way for her to express herself through characters she will, unfortunately, never meet.

82

A Beastly Growl
by Yukari Kousaka

Translated by Toshiya Kamei

A beastly growl comes from behind. Where are you, Father? I click my tongue in despair. While looking for Father, I've gotten lost in the mountains. The growl intensifies to a low rumble. It's a wolf. My heartbeat speeds up, blood pounding in my ears. Instead of panicking, however, I calm myself and listen to the snarl of the beast. Its sporadic growling drives me down the meandering path. After many turns and bends, a familiar opening comes into view. I'm almost home! My mind flashes back to that day Father said, 'An okuri-ōkami escorts you home when you're lost.'

Born in Osaka in 2001, YUKARI KOUSAKA is a Japanese poet, fiction writer, and essayist. Translated by Toshiya Kamei, her short fiction has appeared in New World Writing.

83

Squatter
by Lindsay King-Miller

Her mother's house in the photograph is a magnificent ruin: broken windows, caved-in roof, dead sunflowers slumped over the porch. "I can make it look nicer," the tattoo artist offers, but she shakes her head. She wants to remember it like this. Empty. Destroyed. *Just like you, Mama. Rot in hell.* She smiles at the needle's bite.

After her shower, she runs her fingers over the angry red lines, savouring the sting. Then she looks closer at her reflection.

The front door of the tattooed house stands open. It didn't do that before.

Long, familiar fingers curl around her wrist.

LINDSAY KING-MILLER is the author of Ask A Queer Chick: A Guide to Sex, Love, and Life for Girls who Dig Girls *(Plume, 2016). Her fiction has appeared in the anthologies* The Fiends in the Furrows *(Nosetouch, 2018),* Tiny Nightmares *(Catapult, 2020), and elsewhere. She lives in Denver with her partner and their two children.*

84

Fine With Me
by Julio Rainion

I’ve walked in this house for so long. The creaky floorboards don’t scare me anymore. The mirrors and their distorted reflections of me don’t either.

The creeper that grows too quickly along the outside walls is a friend. I’ve named every blood-red leaf, every tendril that’s strangled unwelcome visitors. I know I’d be the next if I tried to leave, but that’s fine with me.

The electricity is long gone, but I don't need light, the others don't like it. They bite at my legs and extinguish candles when I light them, even now, when my body has long-since withered away.

JULIO RAINION lives in New York with his three cats, his partner, and his dog. When he's not writing, he's usually gardening and trying to find a home for his many spider plants, because he only has so much window space. He has been published in Young Writers Project *and* Speculative 66 *under a different name.*

85

Malachite Shards
by Umiyuri Katsuyama

Translated by Toshiya Kamei

The scent of burning incense filled the air. The smoke wafted over the shelf lined with malachite shards and wrapped around my grandfather's dead body in the tatami room. When he was still alive, he allowed nobody to sleep here. For fear of incurring his ire, nobody dared ask why. While I kept vigil next to his futon, a knock pounded on the front door. I answered it, but nobody was there. Outside, a gale sped through the nocturnal air. When I returned, Grandfather's face had been crushed like a split pomegranate. A blood-drenched malachite shard lay on the floor.

UMIYURI KATSUYAMA is a Japanese writer of fantasy and horror. In 2011, she won the Japan Fantasy Novel Award with her novel Sazanami no kuni. *Her latest novel,* Chuushi, ayashii nabe to tabi wo suru, *was published in 2018. Her short fiction has appeared in numerous horror anthologies in Japan.*

86

Masala
by Anjali Patel

Preeti didn't want to take the satchel of hing to school, but her mother insisted. Just in case, mama said.

Her classmates held their noses as the teacher introduced her. At recess, they ripped the satchel from her pockets, spilling its sulphurous reek across the hot blacktop. They told Preeti to go back to where she came from. She wanted to cry, but didn't. Instead, she crumpled her skirt in her fists and her shadow stepped forward. It leaned toward the children, salivated, multiplied. Her ancestors had fasted since they followed her across the ocean and oh, how they hungered.

ANJALI PATEL is a software engineer and fantasy writer. When her Twitter is active (it usually is not), you can find her at @anjapatel, or view her website and newsletter at https://anjali.fyi/.

87

The Gift
by Elle Jauffret

The house stands in the middle of a manicured lawn like a jagged mount in the middle of the sea.

A priceless inheritance, the attorney appraises.

The girl agrees with a nod. T'was my childhood home.

The building's grey stone, barely visible under the façade-devouring ivy, doesn't belong to her memory, nor does the grand staircase's blood lustre or the blooming wallpaper flowers suffocating the walls. But the smirking old men portraits had been etched in her mind the way her bed's rusty iron chains had scarred her growing wrists and ankles.

Priceless, she says. Burn it to the ground.

ELLE JAUFFRET is a French American writer and Californian attorney who writes across genres. You can find her at ellejauffret.com or on Twitter/Instagram @ellejauffret.

88

The Empty Mirror
by Toshiya Kamei

'Honey, I'm home!' you announce in a singsong tone. However, no reply comes.

Your dog dashes swiftly to the entrance. He pants heavily, his tongue hanging out. Instead of jumping up into your lap, he growls, baring his teeth.

'What's the matter?' your wife booms as she comes down the stairs. 'Hey, there's nobody!' She cuddles the dog before shooing him away. She walks right through you as if you don't exist.

'Hello? Susie, I'm right here!' you yell and frantically wave your arms. You give up. You float through the closed bathroom door and stand before the empty mirror.

TOSHIYA KAMEI's short fiction has appeared in New World Writing.

89

New Holiday Home
by Meera Dandekar

I crouched below the window. The climate was freezing my barely covered limbs. My head popped up just enough to take a look inside the house.

Family was together, without me. How dare they.

Sister was pulling *his* hair. Mother added food to *his* plate. Father was having a laugh with *him*.

I couldn't take it anymore.

I banged on the door and Mother opened it. Shocked to see me, she started to cry. Everyone moved away from me.

I locked my eyes with him. I pulled my knife out. It went through.

I took his place in *his* family.

MEERA DANDEKAR loves to explore the fictional worlds that show the magical realm of being. She's studying mechanical engineering but has a definite admiration for the written word. She's currently living in Mumbai, India.

90

The Good Bones of a Haunted House
by Cara Mast Murray

Look into your ugly places,
open the doors you try to hide,
dig deep and feel the blood and bile and shit coat your hands.

They were already stained.

    You do not scream, it would be impolite,
    so you feast on this misery.

    A meal vile, and rich.
    It tastes like home.

When your ugly makes you sick,
you vomit words
raw and tear-salted.

But the ugly is what brought you up,
fed your soul,
built your bones.

You cannot be and be clean of it.

Swallow your sin

but also,

pry out your strong bones and make something better.

As a retired tall-ship sailor, a failed aspiring academic, and a millennial finance professional, CARA MAST MURRAY is someone who gets stopped constantly in New York City and asked for directions. She spends her free time drinking coffee, binging words, and yelling about the Philadelphia Eagles in her apartment and her family group chat.

91

Happiness in the Cinders
by Micah Castle

Cinders drift through the broken pane, piling on the bowing hardwood. Wind blows, walls creak, soot trickles through the gouge in the roof.

I tinker with father, lining wire down misshapen arms, coiling it around rusted joints. Mother sits across the room, gray wooden limbs splayed in ash. Little sister lies in the corner, head resting on a splintered hand.

I lift his blank face, spit into a handful of dust, and finger paint eyes, a nose, a smile. Tears come and I smear them away.

It only took the world disintegrating for this home to become a happy one.

MICAH CASTLE is a weird fiction and horror writer. His stories have appeared in various places, and he has three collections currently out. He enjoys spending time with his wife, aimlessly hiking through the woods, playing with his animals, and can be found reading a book somewhere in his Pennsylvania home. You can find him on Twitter @micah_castle, Reddit r/MicahCastle, on micahcastle.com and on Amazon: https://www.amazon.com/Micah-Castle/e/B01MRMSB5Y%3Fref=dbs_a_mng_rwt_scns_share.

92

Forever Bad Home
by Thomas Sturgeon Jr.

The former residents left lots of trash from floor to ceiling. This place I called home has been nothing more than a forgotten prison cell as cobwebs litter the entire ceiling. Being forgotten in this place of misery was my shortcoming all along. They say there's no place like home but that's torture to my spectral ears.

They abandoned my body as I was strung out on drugs. The misery I felt still torments as they laugh along their merry way. This place has been condemned for good reason.

Now leave my spirit at peace. Or suffer the consequences.

THOMAS STURGEON JR. is a thirty-four-year-old author living in Chatsworth, Georgia. His stories and poetry have appeared in multiple anthologies. He loves horror stories, movies, and video games. He also has a short story collection called Red Carnival. He loves his family and friends. He also has a cat named Tigger whom he loves dearly.

93

Going Home
by Toshiya Kamei

I kick frantically, trying my darn hardest to stay afloat, as somebody, or something, grabs my ankle and pulls me to the river bottom. I touch floating plants, trying to grab them in vain. I scream inside my head as water fills my nose and mouth. I'm choking. I can't breathe. I can't breathe! Darkness presses heavily over my eyes as memories of home flood my mind. Mom and I baking Christmas cookies. Dad teaching me how to hold a rifle. Steady, boy, steady! When I let out one last breath and shut my eyes one final time, I'm home.

TOSHIYA KAMEI's short fiction has appeared in New World Writing.

94

Hearth and Home
by Gordon B. White

As I steered her towards the grumbling hearth, the purple silk veiling the hole of her face trembled. She hooted like a nightbird: 'So cold, my son. So cold.'

The thing that kept claiming to have been our mother sank onto dirt-caked knees and lamb-white hands, then dutifully crawled inside.

'You must come, too,' she wailed. 'To check the windows and latch the doors.'

I nudged the trim of her funeral clothes inside and closed the grate. An orange tongue licked the damp hem, hissed, then little red teeth bit in.

'This is your little house now, Mother. Stay warm.'

GORDON B. WHITE is the author of the collection As Summer's Mask Slips and Other Disruptions *(Trepidatio Publishing). His stories have appeared in dozens of venues, including* The Best Horror of the Year Vol. 12. *A graduate of the Clarion West Writers Workshop, you can find him online at* gordonbwhite.com *or on Twitter at @GordonBWhite.*

95

Dream House
by Cody Mower

I'm being chased through snow covered forest in the twilight of the night. It sounds like dogs or people, but I can't be sure.

The moon grows bright, casting twisted ribbons of dark on unbroken white, and every time I'm about to become content with dying in the dark, I see a break in the trees and a lone house standing.

Don't open that door.

I know what awaits in the dark.

I can smell the chemicals.

Don't open that door.

But I do.

Again.

And Again.

And Again.

CODY MOWER is a writer from the Maine. After graduating with his B.A. in English, he was accepted into Stonecoast for is MFA creative writing. Most days he can be found either at his desk or wandering aimlessly through the trees.

96

The Inheritance
by H.B. Diaz

The house cast its gloom upon me as I peered into the window, the darkness within malignant, sentient. I wanted no part of this wretched pile of memory and stone, but Father's untimely demise had hurled the horrible structure into my possession. As I looked, I saw his narrow eyes and hooked nose in the filmy glass, but it was not my father who glared back at me. I stared instead at my own reflection.

The truth came into my heart at once, like an iron stake: I had not inherited this house at all, no. It had inherited me.

H.B. DIAZ is a gothic horror writer whose short fiction has been featured in anthologies by Horror Tree, ID Press, Flame Tree Press, and others. She is a member of the Horror Writers Association and lives with her husband and son in a historic (and likely haunted) Maryland town. You can find her on Twitter @hollybdiaz or on Amazon: https://amazon.com/author/hbdiaz.

97

Mirror Mirror
by Mary Rajotte

First, you must drape the fabric tightly. Make sure every inch is obscured. Every mirror and gleaming surface. Windows, too. One cannot be too careful.

If you have no fabric at hand, turn the mirrors to the wall. Keep them that way thereafter.

After taking every precaution, shadows may bloom like spores from dark corners and seep into the cracks and crevices as some *other* thing lingering in the periphery.

Heed it no mind. For the presence that remains will take your notice as an invitation to cling with fingertips, icy and long, to this comforting haunt, this eternal home.

Toronto-native MARY RAJOTTE has a penchant for penning nightmarish tales of folk horror and paranormal suspense. Her work has been published in Shroud Magazine, The Library of Horror Press, The Great Lakes Horror Company, Magnificent Cowlick Media, Fabled Collective *and* Burial Day Books. *Sometimes camera-elusive but always coffee-fuelled, you can find Mary at her website maryrajotte.com or support her Patreon for exclusive fiction at patreon.com/maryrajotte.*

98

this is home
by doungjai gam

The walls whisper in hushed tones. Blood bubbles through the foundation in no discernible pattern. The vines that crawl on the house caress me while I pluck weeds from the beds.

The gardens in the backyard are lush where my dad dropped dead years ago. My mom passed in her sleep shortly afterwards. My brother fell down the cellar stairs—his blood still stains the floor.

I tried to run, but grief is a powerful tether.

My time is here. The walls close in on me, the floor unsteady. I welcome my family's embrace in the darkness, our reunion complete.

doungjai gam is the author of glass slipper dreams, shattered *and* watch the whole goddamned thing burn. *Her work has appeared in* LampLight *and* Cape Cod Poetry Review, *among other places. Born in Thailand, she resides in New England with author Ed Kurtz.*

You can find her on Twitter @djai76 or Facebook: doungjai gam.

99

Only Love Can Hurt Like This
by Antonia Rachel Ward

Your smile caught like a sunbeam on my wall of ice. I couldn't remember the last time I felt warmth, and I tried everything I could to get your attention. Finally, you glanced my way. I wanted to reach out and pull you close. But I died a long time ago. You shivered as you walked through me.

I swore I'd haunt you, but the truth was, you haunted me. I watched you live in my home until I couldn't stand it any longer. I had to find a way to make you mine forever.

We can be ghosts together.

ANTONIA RACHEL WARD is a writer of horror, Gothic and speculative fiction based in Cambridgeshire, UK. Her short stories have been published by Black Hare Press and Friday Flash Fiction. You can find her on Twitter @AntoniaRachelW1, Instagram @antoniarachelward or at antoniarachelward.com.

100

Home in the Reflection of Oblivion
by Alec Thompson

Home...

Thinking this—not so much thinking as feeling an intuition—what once was Stefanie Lyndsey soars through the night sky so clear and sparkling it might be a mirror reflecting back oblivion. Leaving behind the place in the ground, marked by stone.

That was not the place. It was too cold and farrow. A soul such as hers deserves warmth and care and above all else… love.

Through the window, then she's sliding between the sheets. Cosy in her bed, and Trixie the cat leaps and curls into a ball below where her feet would be…

Home... at last.

ALEC THOMPSON lives with his family in Austin, Texas. He holds a BA in Communication Studies from Texas A&M University-Corpus Christi and studied for a MA in Radio, Television, and Film at the University of North Texas. When not writing, he works outdoors for local Parks and Recreation. Follow him on Twitter @aalecthompson.

ACKNOWLEDGEMENTS

Set up a publisher and release a book? It sounded daunting, even to me. But in the course of creating Ghost Orchid Press, I've had the great pleasure of discovering a diverse, supportive, close-knit community of horror writers and readers who have buoyed me up when times got tough. Thank you to everyone who offered advice, assistance, support, and tea and sympathy as needed. And thank you especially to all those who submitted stories. It was a delight to read them all and an honour to have the opportunity to publish them. I appreciate every last one of you.

Much love,

Antonia

ALSO FROM GHOST ORCHID PRESS

Find more terrifying microfiction in *Hundred Word Horror: Beneath.*

https://ghostorchidpress.com

Printed in Great Britain
by Amazon